CLARENCE'S
Topsy-Turvy Shabbat

To Naomi Rivka, who had the idea first.
And to Shmuli—your book is coming.—J.T.M.

For Jasmine and Esme—J.P.

KAR-BEN PUBLISHING, INC.
An imprint of Lerner Publishing Group, Inc.
241 First Avenue North
Minneapolis, MN 55401 USA
1-800-4-KARBEN

Website address: www.karben.com

Main body text set in Zemestro Std
Typeface provided by Monotype Typography

Library of Congress Cataloging-in-Publication Data

Names: MacLeod, Jennifer Tzivia, author. | Poh, Jennie, illustrator.
Title: Clarence's topsy-turvy Shabbat / Jennifer Tzivia MacLeod ; illustrated by
    Jennie Poh.
Description: Minneapolis, MN : Kar-Ben Publishing, [2020] | Series: Shabbat |
    Summary: Neighbors of Clarence the raccoon worry that he is buying all of the
    wrong supplies for his Shabbat Challah, but he has a surprise or two in store
    for them.
Identifiers: LCCN 2019007485| ISBN 9781541542426 (lb : alk. paper) |
    ISBN 9781541542433 (pb : alk. paper)
Subjects: | CYAC: Raccoon—Fiction. | Challah (Bread)—Fiction. | Bread—
    Fiction. | Baking—Fiction. | Sabbath—Fiction. | Judaism—Customs and
    practices—Fiction.
Classification: LCC PZ7.1.M246 Cl 2020 | DDC [E]—dc23

LC record available at https://lccn.loc.gov/2019007485

PJ Library Edition ISBN 978-1-72841-564-2

Manufactured in China
1-48673-49094-10/23/2019

052036.9K1/B1495/A5

CLARENCE'S
Topsy-Turvy Shabbat

Jennifer Tzivia MacLeod

illustrated by Jennie Poh

KAR-BEN
PUBLISHING

Clarence loves Shabbat. All week long he prepares to bake his challah.
On Sunday, he goes out to buy **flour**.
But he comes home with a . . .
FLOWER.

**Oh, no,
Clarence!**

You can't make challah out of
THAT kind of flower.

On Monday, Clarence goes
out to buy **oil**.
But he comes home with . . .
SOIL.

Uh-Oh, Clarence!

Please don't use **THAT** in your challah.

On Tuesday, Clarence goes out to buy **honey**.
But he comes home with a . . .
BUNNY.

Seriously, Clarence?
WHAT are you thinking?

On Wednesday, Clarence goes out to get **water**.
But he comes home with an . . .
OTTER.

Silly Clarence.

You can't keep an otter in the house.
Put him in the pool.
Quickly. Oy, vey!

On Thursday, Clarence goes out to buy **yeast**.

But he comes home with a . . . **BEAST**.

Where on EARTH are you going to put a beast, Clarence? Perhaps try the garage.

It's Friday morning. Shabbat is coming.
Clarence wakes up early.
It is time to make the challah!
Clarence whispers something in the bunny's ear.

Together, they hop next door . . .

. . . and bring back supplies from their friends.

Flour, **oil**, **honey**, and **yeast**.

Did you promise them fresh challah, Clarence? What a good idea.

Clarence whispers something in the otter's ear.

The otter goes to the sink and fills up a measuring cup with cool, fresh water.

Careful, Clarence.

Don't let the otter slip-slide in the dough.
Your friends will **NOT** want otter hairs in
their challah.

Clarence whispers something in the beast's ear. And the beast . . .
Clarence, how did you know?

The beast is absolutely terrific at kneading
challah dough.

Its arms never get tired.
Clarence puts the
challah into the oven.

It's starting to **smell delicious** in here, Clarence!

In the corner of the room, next to the bag of soil, the flower is drooping. Clarence takes the dirt and droopy plant outside . . .

. . . and comes back with a **beautiful** flower for the Shabbat table.

On Friday night, Clarence's friends behave themselves nicely.

Clarence says the blessings over the candles and wine. He says the prayer over the bread and shares the delicious, fresh challah.

I told you it would be a wonderful Shabbat, Clarence.

What? I didn't tell you?
Well, I thought so all along.
I really did.

Clarence leans across the Shabbat table and whispers something in my ear.

What's that, Clarence?

No, don't tell me what you're planning for next Shabbat. Let's keep it a surprise, okay?